This book belongs to

Eric Remillard

from Gramma & Granpa Stairs

The Not-So-Perfect Picnic

Published by Advance Publishers
www.advance-publishers.com

Written by Greg Ehrbar
Illustrated by Adrienne Brown and Brian Sebern
Editorial development and management by Bumpy Slide Books
Illustrations produced by Disney Publishing Creative Development
Cover design by Deborah Boone

ISBN: 1-57973-027-2

It was early Monday morning. Atta was trying to
meet with Thorny, but several ants kept interrupting
them.

"Princess Atta!" called one of the ants.

"I have a question, Your Highness!" called
Dr. Flora.

"If you'll all please wait your turn," said Atta.

"Atta!" Dot cried impatiently.

But Princess Atta didn't answer. Her head was already aching. She needed a break.

"Atta!" Dot cried again. "What can I do to help?"
Atta sighed. "I just don't know," she answered
wearily.

Atta leaned against a mushroom. "How will I ever manage when I'm queen someday?"

"Maybe you just need a day off, Your Majesty!" said Flik. He was perched on top of the mushroom. "I know a place where you can rest."

"A day off?" Cornelius said sternly. "How silly! Even I have never taken a day off!"

"Besides," Thorny added, "Flik's ideas always turn into disasters!"

"Thorny's right!" Cornelius concluded.

"Nuh-uh!" Dot argued. "Flik's right! Go on,
Atta. I'll help Mom run things while you're gone."

Atta smiled gratefully.

"I'm glad you're going," the Queen told Atta. "It will be a good chance for me to start training Dot." Before Atta even knew what was happening, the Queen had ordered her subjects to pack a tasty picnic lunch. Soon Flik and Atta were on their way.

"Just follow me, Princess," Flik said, as the pair headed away from the anthill. "We are going to have one fun-filled, relaxing day!"

Flik continued to chatter happily as the two walked along. "Now, isn't this a pretty trail?" he asked proudly. He turned to face Atta while he spoke.

"And—AAHHH!" screamed Flik as he and Atta tumbled into a bog.

"Sorry, Princess Atta!" cried Flik. "I, uh . . ."

But Atta was laughing!
"It's okay," she said. "I always love a nice, cool dip!"
Besides, she knew her friend meant well.

By the time the two reached the bank, they were muddier than ever. Flik made a shower by poking holes in a leaf full of dew.

"Whew! Thanks, Flik," Atta gurgled. "Maybe we should turn back, though. I have lots to do."

"Oh, not yet! Please, Princess!" said Flik. "I think we're almost there!"

They walked on. Moments later, they came
to a clearing.

"Surprise!" announced Flik happily. "Here's our
picnic spot!"

"How lovely!" said Atta. "Our own private beach!"
Flik quickly folded a leaf into a comfy chair for
the princess.

"Please have a seat, Your Majesty," he said.

Flik busied himself fixing some food for Atta. But when he turned to serve it to her, she was gone!

"Princess Atta!" called Flik.

"Under here," came a muffled voice. Atta's chair had collapsed on her!

"I'm so sorry!" cried Flik as he untangled Atta.

Atta couldn't help laughing. "My goodness! Resting sure is hard work!" she joked.

"Hold on! I have another surprise for you!"
Flik said.

"What is it?" asked Atta.

"You'll see," teased Flik. Then he set to work.

In a few minutes, Flik had made a beautiful umbrella from wildflower petals. "Ta-da!" he exclaimed. "It's to shade you from the sun."

The princess was amazed—and touched. "Oh, Flik!" she said with a smile.

Suddenly a gust of wind kicked up. It blew away the umbrella—and carried off the food!

Flik thought Atta would never want to go out with him again.

But Atta wasn't upset at all! "Well, it was a nice umbrella while it lasted!" she giggled.

The sky darkened. The wind blew harder.

"This has been fun," Atta said. "But I'm worried about the colony. Would you mind if we started home?"

Flik sighed. "I understand," he said.

The two ants struggled against the howling wind. Soon it was whirling them off their feet.

"We sure could use a good idea right now!" Atta called, grabbing onto a piece of grass.

"Hang on, Princess!" Flik said.
Thinking quickly, Flik made a small shelter.

After Atta was safe, he went outside to gather some berries growing nearby. Soon he and Atta were feasting on the juicy fruit.

Later, Flik played Atta his favorite lullaby.
"My mother used to sing that to me," said
Atta dreamily.

The music from Flik's flute drifted over her until she was fast asleep.

When Atta awoke, she saw Flik making small repairs to the shelter.

"I hope I didn't disturb you," Flik said. "I'm sorry this day didn't turn out as well as I had hoped."

"No, Flik. It was a wonderful day," Atta told him. "I wouldn't have had it any other way, or with anyone else but you."

Flik blushed. "Maybe we should go home now."

"There you are!" said the Queen as Flik and Atta returned to the colony. "We were safe in the anthill during the storm, but how did you do?"

"We fell in the mud, our lunch got ruined, and we nearly blew away!" Atta explained.

Embarrassed, Flik wished he could disappear.

"I knew Flik would mess up," said Thorny.

"Flik did not mess up!" Atta corrected. "He solved every problem cleverly. I never had so much fun in my life."

The Queen and Dot grinned. The other ants were amazed.

"Thanks for such a relaxing day, Flik," said Atta. "Now I can't wait to get back to work!"

Flik beamed with pride. "You're welcome, Princess. May we do it again soon?"

"Well, maybe someday," Atta replied. "Only next time, let's check the weather first!"

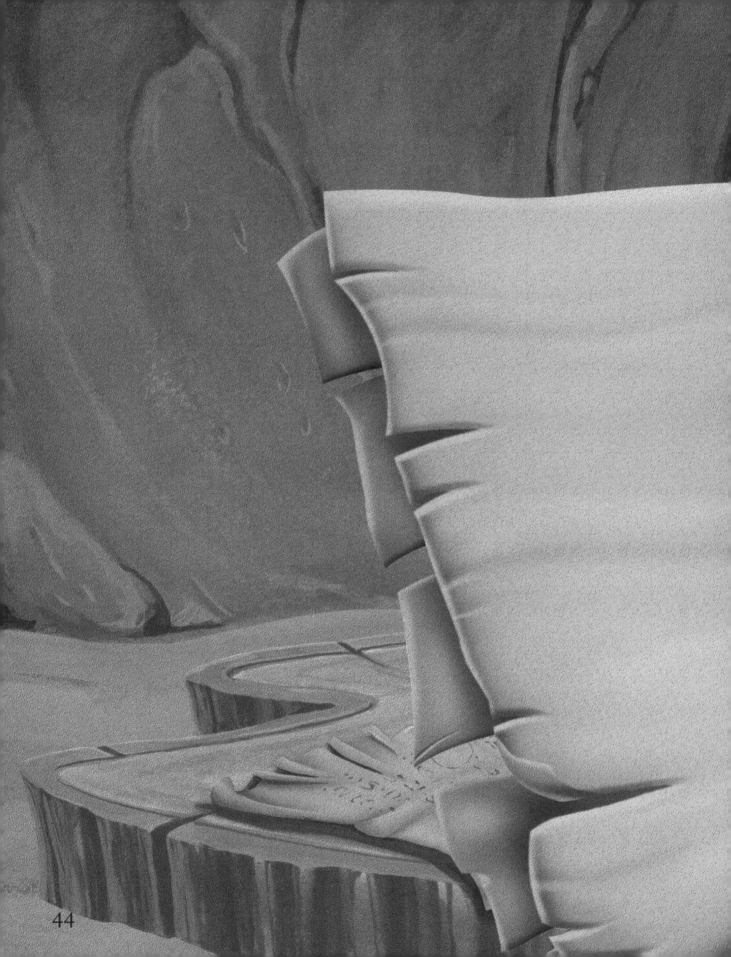

Dear Blueberry Journal,

My sister Atta likes to rest after a busy day of training to be queen. My mom says rest is good for ants. My friends and I like to snuggle deep in the anthill and sleep. When we sleep a really long time, it's called hibernation.

Caterpillars go to sleep wrapped up in something called a cocoon. After a long while, they come out as beautiful butterflies!

Flik told me there are even some bugs, like locusts, that sleep for years and years. I'm glad we don't have to sleep that long. There are too many fun things to do!

Till next time,
Dot